THIEVES' WORLD

GRAPHICS **2**

Adapted and Scripted
By Robert Lynn Asprin and Lynn Abbey

Artwork by Tim Sale   Edited by Laurie Sutton

Publisher Liaison—Kay Reynolds

STARBLAZE GRAPHICS

Starblaze Graphics—The Donning Company/Publishers
Norfolk/Virginia Beach • 1986

Look for further volumes of **Thieves' World Graphics** to be published · quarterly. This is only one of many graphic novels and series published by The Donning Company/Publishers. For a complete listing of our titles, please write to the address below.

The Donning Company/Publishers
5659 Virginia Beach Boulevard
Norfolk, Virginia 23502

10 9 8 7 6 5 4 3 2 1

Library of Congress Cataloging-in-Publication Data

Asprin, Robert.
  Thieves' world graphics #2.
  I. Abbey, Lynn. II. Sale, Tim. III. Title:
Thieves' world graphics number two.
PS3551.S6T54   1986   813'.54   85-20471
ISBN 0-89865-415-5 (pbk.)

Printed in the United States of America

THIEVES' WORLD GRAPHICS

Featuring characters and stories created by:

Lynn Abbey

Poul Anderson

Robert Lynn Asprin

Robin Bailey

John Brunner

C. J. Cherryh

Christine DeWees

David Drake

Diane Duane

Philip Jose Farmer

Joe Haldeman

Vonda McIntyre

Chris & Janet Morris

Andrew J. Offutt

Diana Paxson

A. E. Van Vogt

Thieves' World Graphics is a continuing series of graphic novels published quarterly and based on the Thieves' World anthologies published by Ace Books.

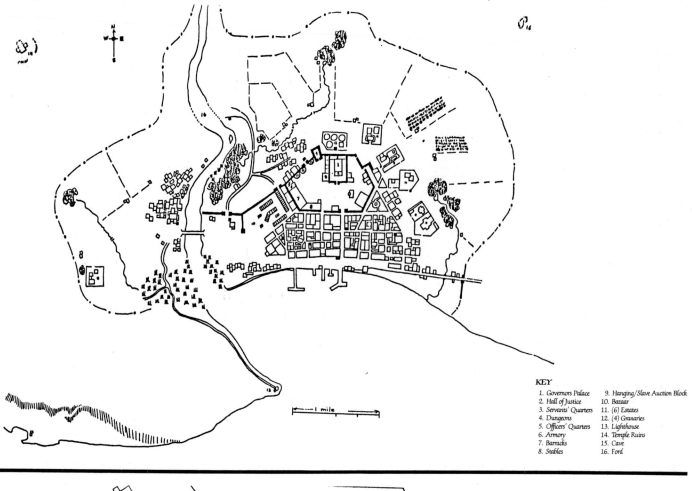

KEY

1. Governors Palace	9. Hanging/Slave Auction Block
2. Hall of Justice	10. Bazaar
3. Servants' Quarters	11. (6) Estates
4. Dungeons	12. (4) Granaries
5. Officers' Quarters	13. Lighthouse
6. Armory	14. Temple Ruins
7. Barracks	15. Cave
8. Stables	16. Ford

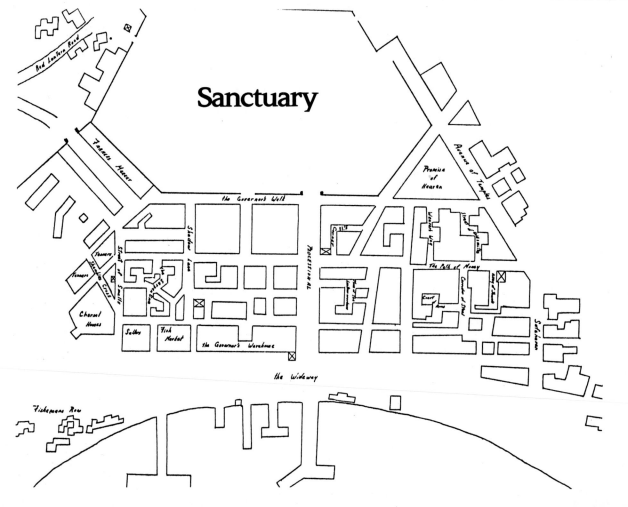

Sanctuary

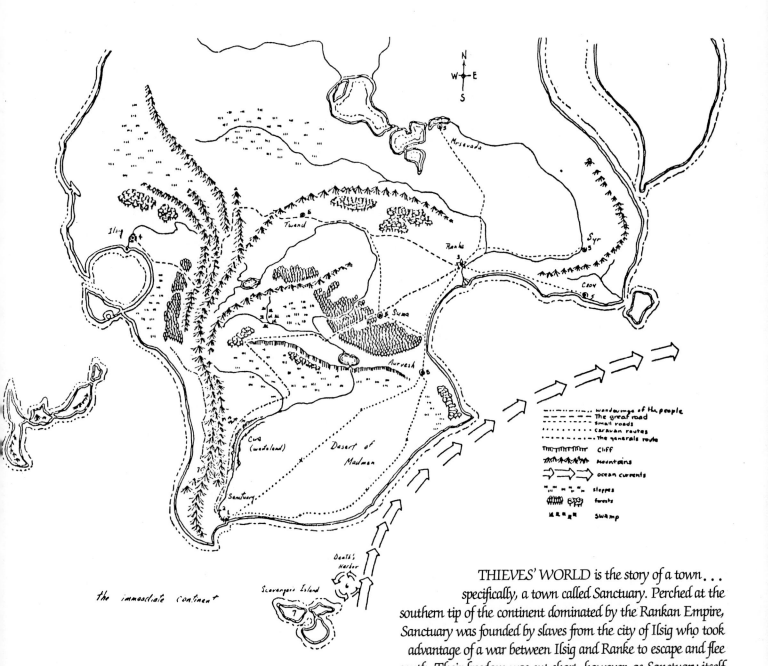

the immediate Continent

Legend:
- - - - - wanderings of the people
——— The great road
——— small roads
· · · · · caravan routes
- · - · - The generals route
⌢⌢⌢⌢ Cliff
🜪🜪🜪 Mountains
⇒⇒⇒ ocean currents
" " " " steppes
🌲🌲 forests
⬚⬚⬚ swamp

THIEVES' WORLD is the story of a town . . . specifically, a town called Sanctuary. Perched at the southern tip of the continent dominated by the Rankan Empire, Sanctuary was founded by slaves from the city of Ilsig who took advantage of a war between Ilsig and Ranke to escape and flee south. Their freedom was cut short, however, as Sanctuary itself was conquered by the Empire and used as a caravan stop between Ranke and the now-defeated city of Ilsig.

Sanctuary prospered until Ranke succeeded in putting down the last stronghold of resistance and opened up a shorter, northern mountain route between the two cities. Now forgotten and unwanted, Sanctuary has fallen on hard times. Those who were able have moved on to more profitable cities, leaving the town to the desperate and petty criminals who have come to use it as a refuge . . . people more concerned with survival than morals.

The most interesting stories are often not about heroes or wielders of power, but about everyday folk. Like people of any era, a majority of the citizens' time is spent trying to earn or steal enough to keep food on the table and a roof overhead. In a town like Sanctuary, however, the simple process of earning a living can be dangerous, and sometimes fatal. . . .

1

2

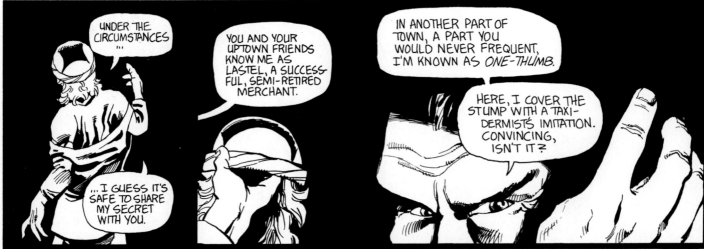

4

FOR THOSE OF LESSER MEANS AND *HIGHER* SCRUPLES, THE SOLUTION TO THEIR PROBLEMS IS NOT ALWAYS SO EASY.

SWEETMEATS!

ALWAYS THE BEST IN THE BAZAAR!

ALWAYS THE BEST IN SANCTUARY!

SWEETMEATS!

AGAIN! I'D HOPED TO PURGE MYSELF OF THIS FEELING OF FOREBODING, BUT INSTEAD...

...WHAT ?

SWEETMEATS!

ace of Chaos

HERE, HAAKON! I'D LIKE TWO...

...NO, WHY DON'T YOU MAKE IT THREE, AND JOIN US FOR BREAKFAST?

THANKS, ILLYRA, I WOULD LOVE TO.

ALWAYS GLAD TO SHARE WITH FOLKS HERE AT THE BAZAAR, AND AT REASONABLE PRICES, TOO. NOT LIKE WHAT I CHARGE THOSE UPTOWN FOLKS THAT DON'T KNOW WHAT TO DO WITH THEIR MONEY.

I WISH I COULD TALK TO DUBRO, BUT HE DISLIKES DEALING WITH MAGIC, INCLUDING MY CARDS.

MUST WORK NOW!

CLINGCLING CLINGCLANG

WE'LL GET IT FIXED, DUBRO! I CAN BORROW MOONFLOWER'S CART, AND...

THEN WE'LL GET A NEW ONE!

HUSH, ILLYRA! YOU CAN'T FIX AN ANVIL WHEN IT'S BROKEN LIKE THAT. IT WOULD ONLY BE AS STRONG AS THE SEAM.

YOU COULDN'T AFFORD IT. AND EVEN IF YOU COULD, IT WOULD TAKE OVER A YEAR TO IMPORT ONE FROM RANKE.

WE'VE GOT TO HAVE ONE!

WITHOUT IT, DUBRO IS...

DUBRO....!

7

EVEN FOR THOSE WITH REGULAR WORK, EARNING A LIVING IN SANCTUARY ISN'T EASY.

INTERRUPTED READINGS... CUSTOMERS WHO WON'T PAY... I NEVER REALIZED HOW MUCH I COUNT ON DUBRO.

BARELY INTO THE HEAT OF THE DAY AND ALREADY THINGS HAVE GONE BADLY FOR ILLYRA. FOR THE FIRST TIME IN FIVE YEARS DUBRO IS NOT THERE TO WATCH THE CURTAIN.

DISRUPTION FROM WITHOUT... THE PROMISE OF THE *FACE OF CHAOS* IS CERTAINLY FULFILLED.

AND NOW THIS... THE *FIVE OF SHIPS* IN RESPONSE TO MY OWN QUESTIONS.

I'VE GOT TO *THINK!*

QUIT WORRYING ABOUT DUBRO AND *CONCENTRATE!*

MADAME ILLYRA?

MADAME?

NOT ANOTHER ONE...

COME BACK TOMORROW.

BUT IT CAN'T WAIT! I NEED YOUR HELP!

THEY ALL SAY THAT. I NEED TIME...

THAT SOUND!

THOSE ARE *SILK* SKIRTS UNDER THAT ROBE. AND SILK MEANS MONEY!

10

YOU DO WHAT? ROACHING?

SHADOWSPAWN, WHAT'S 'ROACHING'?

SHHH... WHEN DO ROACHES COME OUT?

WHY,.. AT NIGHT.

AND SO DO THIEVES.

OH, HANSE, YOU KNOW JUST ABOUT *EVERYTHING*, DON'T YOU?

THE STREETS ARE MY HOME. THEY BIRTHED ME; RAISED ME.

I KNOW QUITE A BIT.

HANSE THE ROACH COULD SCARCELY BELIEVE HIS LUCK: TO BE HERE — RATHER THAN DRINKING IN THE MAZE. WITH A GENUINELY BEAUTIFUL WOMAN — AND ONE OF THE PRINCE'S CONCUBINES. TO HAVE HER ADMIRATION — AND A CHANCE FOR REVENGE!

THEY'RE EYE-CATCHING, AREN'T THEY?

IN RANKE I'D HAVE TO HIDE THEM BENEATH HIGH-NECKED HOMESPUN.

UH,.. WELL, LIRAIN... THOSE PEARLS...

BUT NOT EVEN *HANSE* BELIEVED HIS INTEREST WAS PURELY PROFESSIONAL.

YOU'RE SO CUTE WHEN YOU *LIE*, HANSE. I GET SO BORED AT THE PALACE...

...CAN'T WE GO SOME PLACE PRIVATE?

ANOTHER WORLD LIES BELOW THE STREETS.

ONE MAN WALKS ITS PATHWAYS — ALONE AND UNAFRAID.

SANCTUARY IS HIS HOME — THE ONLY PLACE WHERE THE MAN KNOWN TO SOME AS LASTEL THE NOBLE-MAN AND MOST AS ONE-THUMB, THE VULGAR UNICORN'S OWNER, CAN LIVE A *NORMAL* LIFE.

HIS DAILY WALK TAKES HIM TO THE LILY GARDEN WHERE HE IS KNOWN — BUT NOT AS A PATRON. VIOLENCE IS THE STARCH OF HIS LUST — BUT NEVER WITH CONSENT.

PASSING THROUGH EARLY TODAY, ONE-THUMB.

MY TAVERN NEEDS A SURPRISE VISIT.

AND TELL AMOLI I'VE GOT SOME-THING FOR HER.

LET ME GUESS!

YOU COULD BUY A PINCH.

THE BEST *KRFF* IN CARONNE... NOW IN SANCTUARY.

A MAN WITHOUT SCRUPLES WOULD KILL YOU FOR IT.

I'M *DOUBLY* SAFE WITH YOU, THEN.

SAFE, IT'S TRUE. ONLY A STRANGER WOULD ATTACK YOU.

FOR EVERYONE KNOWS ONE-THUMB'S PROTECTION: A WELL-MAINTAINED CURSE CONSIGNING HIS MURDERER TO AN ETERNITY OF BURNING.

BUT SHOULD WE PITY ANYONE ATTACKING THE NOBLEMAN KNOWN AS LASTEL?

15

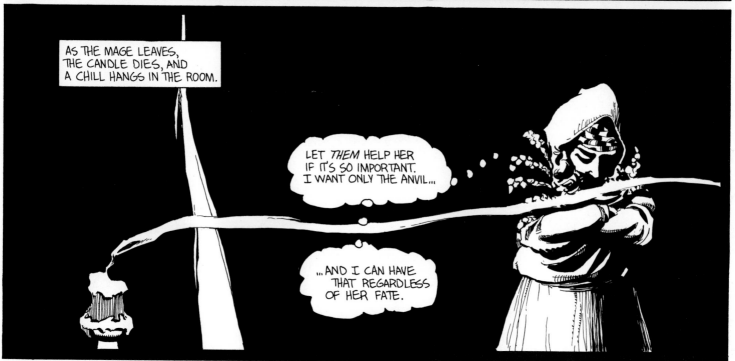

WHAT WAS THE MEANING OF THE ENCOUNTER ILLYRA HAD NEARLY INTERRUPTED AT MOONFLOWER'S?

THEY'RE BEAUTIFUL, HANSE.

AND ONLY A SMALL PART OF THE AFTERNOON'S PLEASURE

THE S'DANZO TUCKS THE PEARLS SAFELY AWAY IN HER 'TREASURE CHEST'

YOU'RE SUCH A GOOD BOY...

ONLY WHEN I WANT SOMETHING, PASSIONFLOWER.

I MET SOMEONE TODAY. SHE PROPOSED SOME BUSINESS.

IT SOUNDS VERY EASY AND VERY PROFITABLE.

AND I'M NOT SURE I TRUST IT.

SHE GAVE ME THIS... FOR SERVICES ALREADY RENDERED.

AHH... I UNDERSTAND.

LET'S SEE WHAT SHE'S LEFT ON IT.

LIKE A GROSS KITTEN, THE SEERESS PLAYS WITH THE SILK.

AND SOON THE VISIONS COME TO HER.

18

19

USE ME, WILL THEY? I'LL USE *THEM* INSTEAD.

I'LL PLAY THEIR GAME AND LET THEM GET ME INTO THE PALACE.

I'LL STEAL THE SAVANKH THAT LETS HIM CONDEMN A MAN TO HANG.

AND HE'LL HAVE TO BUY IT BACK FROM ME FOR GOLD—

—NO, *SILVER*, IT'S EASIER TO CHANGE.

AND WHEN I'M SAFE AWAY I'LL LET HIM KNOW HOW I DID IT—

AND THE WOMAN WHO GAVE ME THE IDEA.

MAYBE I'LL EVEN GO TO RANKE AND TELL THE EMPEROR.

LET HIM KNOW *ONE* IL SIGI THIEF IS SMARTER, CLEVERER, THAN A *DOZEN* OF HIS OWN.

LATER, IN A MISTY TWILIGHT, SANCTUARY'S SMALL HANDFUL OF POWERFUL MEN AND WOMEN GATHER FOR AN EVENING OF ENTERTAINMENT AND WHISPERS AT THE SURPRISINGLY LUXURIOUS HOME OF TASFALEN LANCOTHIS.

SO THEY FOUND AMAR'S SIGNET-RING IN A HONEYPOT BUT NO SIGN OF *HIM* — NOT EVEN A BODY? USUALLY THERE'S A BODY, EVEN *HERE*, LORD TORCHHOLDER.

STRANGE, LANCOTHIS, I HAD THOUGHT NOTHING WAS UNUSUAL HERE.

THAT LOOKS DANGEROUS.

I THINK HE'D BE RATHER INTERESTING...

AFTER A PROPER BATH, OF COURSE.

YOU'LL HAVE TO TAKE STEPS. NOT EVEN THE PRINCE WOULD DARE TO PUT THE BITE ON THE CARAVAN TARIFFS.

THE FIRST STEPS HAVE ALREADY BEEN TAKEN.

I TOLD YOU THE LITTLE THIEF'S TAKEN THE BAIT.

SO LONG AS THAT'S ALL HE'S TAKEN.

HE HAS HIS CHARMS— BUT HE'S A PREDICTABLE FOOL.

AND AS THE PARTY DRAWS TO AN END...

THE PRICE WAS THREE RANKAN SILVERS!

FOR ENTERTAINMENT, I WAS NOT IMPRESSED. MY GUESTS WERE *BORED*.

BE THANKFUL I DO NOT ASK *YOU* TO PAY FOR THE FOOD YOUR CHILDREN STOLE....

MY CHILDREN DO NOT STEAL!

I SAID I WOULD NOT CHARGE YOU— DON'T PRESS YOUR LUCK FURTHER.

CHARISART! MOSSIKER! SHOW THIS SCUM TO THE STREET!

UNGFH!

DUBRO! NO-O-O!

FORGETTING CAUTION, ILLYRA RUNS TOWARDS THE FALLEN TORCH...

SWEET MERCY, IT'S ONE OF JUBAL'S HAWKMASKS...

...BUT IN SANCTUARY, JUSTICE WEARS A FEARSOME FACE.

ILLYRA WATCHES IN HORROR AS EACH MAN IN HIS TURN TAKES THE KNIFE AND STRIKES THE CORPSE AGAIN AND AGAIN.

THEY GET ROBBED TOO.

IT'S JUSTICE... I GUESS.

A MAN'S DEEDS MUST CATCH UP WITH HIM...

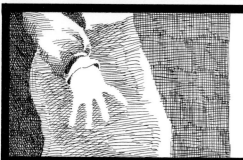

23

THE STORY OF THE HAWKMASK'S DEATH FALLS FROM HER IN SOBS...

...AND WITH THE FIRST TOUCH OF HER TEARS ON HIS CHEST, DUBRO KNOWS SHE HAS SUFFERED TOO MUCH IN HIS ABSENCE.

IT'S A SLOW NIGHT AT THE VULGAR UNICORN.

THE QUIET SUITS ONE-THUMB. THERE'LL BE BUSINESS TRANSACTED UPSTAIRS TONIGHT WHERE THE KRFF IS LOCKED AWAY, AND THE FEWER INQUISITIVE EYES, THE BETTER.

UNGFH!

DUBRO! NO-O-O!

FORGETTING CAUTION, ILLYRA RUNS TOWARDS THE FALLEN TORCH...

SWEET MERCY, IT'S ONE OF JUBAL'S HAWKMASKS...

THEY GET ROBBED TOO.

IT'S JUSTICE... I GUESS.

A MAN'S DEEDS MUST CATCH UP WITH HIM...

...BUT IN SANCTUARY, JUSTICE WEARS A FEARSOME FACE.

ILLYRA WATCHES IN HORROR AS EACH MAN IN HIS TURN TAKES THE KNIFE AND STRIKES THE CORPSE AGAIN AND AGAIN.

THE STORY OF THE HAWKMASK'S DEATH FALLS FROM HER IN SOBS...

...AND WITH THE FIRST TOUCH OF HER TEARS ON HIS CHEST, DUBRO KNOWS SHE HAS SUFFERED TOO MUCH IN HIS ABSENCE.

IT'S A SLOW NIGHT AT THE VULGAR UNICORN.

THE QUIET SUITS ONE-THUMB. THERE'LL BE BUSINESS TRANSACTED UPSTAIRS TONIGHT WHERE THE *KRFF IS* LOCKED AWAY. AND THE FEWER INQUISITIVE EYES, THE BETTER.

IT IS LATER THAN HE EXPECTS, BUT THEY FINALLY COME THROUGH THE DOOR.

AMOLI, MISTRESS OF THE LILY GARDEN, AND HER EUNUCH BODYGUARD.

NOT OUT HERE. I'VE GOT A PRIVATE TABLE, IN THE BACK.

KELEM SAYS YOU'VE GOT A FULL BLOCK OF CARONNE FOR SALE.

PRIME AND PURE.

THAT'S A LOT.

HOW DID YOU GET IT?

I'D RATHER NOT SAY.

YOU'D BETTER SAY. I HAD SUCH A BLOCK IN MY STRONG-BOX UNTIL YESTERDAY WHEN SOMEONE STOLE IT.

AN INTERESTING COINCIDENCE.

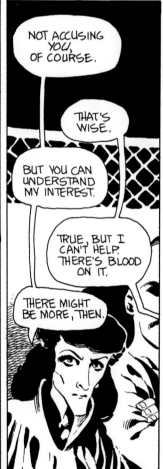

NOT ACCUSING YOU, OF COURSE.

THAT'S WISE.

BUT YOU CAN UNDERSTAND MY INTEREST.

TRUE, BUT I CAN'T HELP. THERE'S BLOOD ON IT.

THERE MIGHT BE MORE, THEN.

GO AHEAD.

I'LL EVEN GIVE YOU MY KNIFE.

WHAT HAPPENS TO YOU WILL BE RATHER WORSE THAN GOING WITHOUT KRFF.

25

IT'S... IT'S NOT FOR ME. I'VE GOT ALMOST EVERYTHING INVESTED IN THAT BLOCK. I'VE GOT TO GET IT BACK.

AND I HOPE YOU DO, BUT IT'S NOT MY BLOCK.

NO? LET ME JUDGE THAT. HAVE YOU HAD IT OVER TWO DAYS?

NO — BUT IT HAD BEEN INSIDE A CARAVAN CHEESE LONGER THAN THAT.

HUMPF. WHO DELIVERED IT?

MARYPE, THE YOUNGEST SON OF MY SORCEROR. HE'S GOOD WITH ANIMALS.

AND THE SMELL OF ROTTING CHEESE.

HE DELIVERED MINE NOT TWO HOURS AFTER THE CARAVAN ARRIVED.

POINT GIVEN. I DIDN'T GET MINE 'TIL EVENING.

SORCERY? NO, HE'S NOT THAT GOOD.

ILLUSION? I TESTED MINE.

I DID TOO. BELOW THE SEAL— WHERE I ALWAYS DO.

WE'LL SETTLE IT. YOU CAN CHECK MY BLOCK.

AND SO...

DAMN THEM ALL TO THE FIRE.

DOES MARYPE? COULD HE... WITHOUT HIS FATHER, I MEAN.

NO, AMOLI. IT WAS THE FATHER WHO DID THIS.

MIZRAITH, WHOSE REPUTATION IS OLDER THAN THE RANKAN PRESENCE IN SANCTUARY, KEEPS TO HIMSELF IN OPULENT QUARTERS ABOVE THE WIDEWAY.

THE STRAIN OF HOLDING HIS MYRIAD SPELLS UNDER CONTROL HAS MADE IT UNWISE FOR HIM TO APPEAR ON THE STREETS. BUT NOT EVEN SHADOW-SPAWN WILL BRAVE HIS UN-SHUTTERED WINDOWS.

FATHER AWAITS YOU UPSTAIRS.

YOU WILL LEAVE YOUR WEAPONS HERE.

STEFAB WAVES HIS HAND AND HIDDEN STEEL GROWS WARM.

WHILE KELEM DISARMS AND ONE-THUMB LIGHT-ENS HIS BOOTS, BELT AND TUNIC, AMOLI TURNS ASIDE AND REACHES HIGH UNDER HER SKIRTS...

HE LEAVES THEM IN HIS FATHER'S WELL-DEFENDED PRESENCE.

HOW GOOD TO SEE YOU, LASTEL — OR WHATEVER YOU CALL YOURSELF THESE DAYS.

YOU'VE BROUGHT ME A PRESENT?

SHE'S TOO OLD FOR YOU, EH?

I'VE BROUGHT YOU BRANDY... AND A COMPLAINT.

THIS WOMAN AND I... WE BELIEVE YOU'VE WRONGED AND CHEATED US.

CALM YOURSELF, SPIRIT.

THESE ARE YET MY FRIENDS.

SERVE YOURSELF FIRST, LASTEL.

THREE GLASSES AND A TABLE APPEAR.

CHEATED YOU? MY, OH MY.

WHAT COULD *YOU* HAVE THAT *I* NEED?

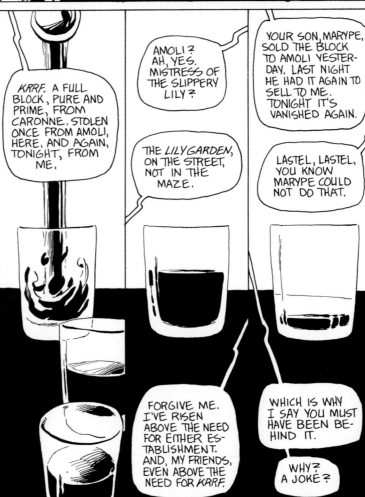

KRRF. A FULL BLOCK, PURE AND PRIME, FROM CARONNE. STOLEN ONCE FROM AMOLI, HERE, AND AGAIN, TONIGHT, FROM ME.

AMOLI? AH, YES. MISTRESS OF THE SLIPPERY LILY?

THE *LILY GARDEN*, ON THE STREET, NOT IN THE MAZE.

YOUR SON, MARYPE, SOLD THE BLOCK TO AMOLI YESTERDAY. LAST NIGHT HE HAD IT AGAIN TO SELL TO ME. TONIGHT IT'S VANISHED AGAIN.

LASTEL, LASTEL, YOU KNOW MARYPE COULD NOT DO THAT.

FORGIVE ME. I'VE RISEN ABOVE THE NEED FOR EITHER ESTABLISHMENT. AND, MY FRIENDS, EVEN ABOVE THE NEED FOR *KRRF*.

WHICH IS WHY I SAY YOU MUST HAVE BEEN BEHIND IT.

WHY? A JOKE?

WOULD YOU LIKE SOME TEA?

NO, MIZRAITH, PLEASE...

LISTEN TO ME.

THIS IS FINANCIAL RUIN FOR AMOLI AND A GROSS INSULT TO ME.

CLAP!

A JOKE, EH? YOU THINK I PASS THE TIME MAKING STUPID JOKES?

28

29

I'M SORRY, THERE'S NOT MUCH OF IT LEFT.

HE SAYS IT'S AS PURE AS YOU PROMISED.

MIZRAITH TAKES THE DUST, INHALES IT, AND SEEKS NOT THE DRUG'S EXHILARATION BUT OTHER KNOWLEDGE.

MARKMOR!

YOUR SON'S IN LEAGUE WITH YOUR COMPETITION?

IN LEAGUE OR IN THRALL.

THE MAGICIAN STANDS AND GESTURES,

-AND IS REPLACED BY THE HIGH-CEILINGED, BUT MORE SPARTAN FURNISHINGS OF A MAGE'S WORKROOM.

THE PLEASURE DOME SHIMMERS —

MUMBLING TO HIMSELF, MIZRAITH INVOKES HIS POWER.

31

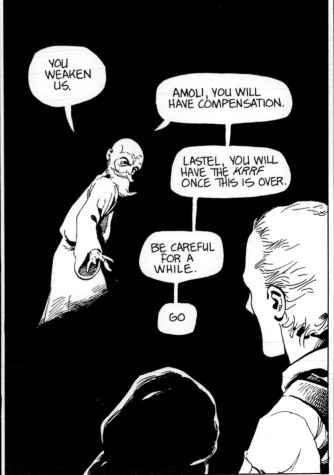

THE PALACE, LATE THAT NIGHT, SHROUDED WITH FOG.

THERE HAD BEEN NO GUARD AT THE GATE, AS LIRAIN HAD PROMISED.

IT MIGHT HAVE BEEN SAFE TO FOLLOW THE REST OF THEIR PLAN AS WELL.

HE'D NEVER KNOW.

IT WAS ENOUGH THAT THE *SAVANKH* RESTED IN IT'S PROPER PLACE.

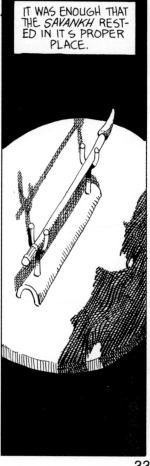

SHALPA'S CLOAK...

IT'S NOTHING BUT AN IVORY TWIG. I'VE SEEN BETTER WORK IN THE BAZAAR!

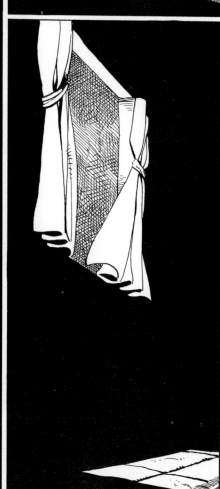

33

34

35

JUBAL HAS RECLAIMED HIS HENCHMAN...

...THEY HAVE NO CHOICE BUT TO VISIT THE PUBLIC GALLOWS.

WHICH ONE?

FATHER

THE LAW SAYS: HUNG IN THE SQUARE UNTIL SUNDOWN.

IT'S A LONG WALK HOME AND BACK...

UNTIL SUNDOWN, PEON.

BUT HE'S DEAD *NOW.*

I NEED SOME- ONE MY SIZE AND BLONDE. *NONE* OF THEM ARE RIGHT.

BEGGARS CAN'T BE CHOOSERS, 'LYRA.

THERE'S LAW NOW.

AT SUNDOWN.

NO EXCEPTIONS.

HOW WILL I MARK SUNDOWN IN ALL THIS RAIN?

≡SIGH≡ ALL RIGHT. CUT HIM DOWN.

WHERE NOW?

HE'S— HE'S—

A CORPSE.

HE *REEKS.*

IT'S THE WAY OF MEN WHO HAVE BEEN HUNG.

THE STORM INTENSIFIES, BATTERING SANCTUARY WITH MINDLESS FURY. FOR ONCE THE STREETS ARE DESERTED AND ALL FACE A COMMON ENEMY.

LITTLE CHAM'S NOT CRYING ANYMORE, ADITI...

... IS HE GETTING BETTER?

NO MARKET AT THE BAZAAR; NO MONEY. IF IT RAINS TO-MORROW, WHAT THEN?

AS THE GODS WILL, SON-IN-LAW. WHEN IT'S OVER THEY'LL NEED HANDS AND BACKS TO REPAIR THE DAMAGES

AND SELL OURSELVES INTO SLAVERY FOR FOOD.

MAYBE THE STORM'LL SEND A SHIP ONTO THE ROCKS AN' WE'LL LOOT IT LIKE PIRATES.

38

40

42

AND SUDDENLY THE RAIN STOPS AGAIN...

YOU'VE COME TO COLLECT YOUR REWARD?

ENAS YORL—! WHAT'S HAPPENED?

WHERE'S MARILLA AND HER FAMILY?

THE HOODED MAGICIAN GESTURES TOWARD THE TUMBLED STONES OF AN OLD GRAVEYARD.

THE PRIESTS OF ILS CREATED THE HOMUNCULUS. IF IT HAD BEEN INTERRED BENEATH THE CORNERSTONE, VASHANKA'S ANGER WOULD HAVE REACHED ACROSS THE DESERT—

AND THE RANKAN GODS WOULD BE WEAKENED, AS THE ILSIG PRIESTS AND THEIR GODS WISHED.

WE MAGICIANS, AND EVEN YOU S'DANZO, DO NOT NEED DIVINE FEUDS. THEY DISRUPT FATE'S BALANCE. OUR WORK IS MORE IMPORTANT THAN THEIRS...

..., SO, AS IN THE PAST, WE INTERVENED.

BUT,.. BUT HE WAS A THIEF, NOT A VIRGIN!

JUST AS THE "VIRGIN" BENEATH ILS CORNERSTONE WAS ONLY A TOOTHLESS CRONE.

SO THE GODS ARE EQUAL?

EQUALLY HANDICAPPED — IN SANCTUARY.

AND WHAT OF ME?

YOU SAID EARLIER...

HAVE I NOT SAID OUR PURPOSE WAS ACHIEVED?

YOU DID NOT FAIL...

...AND WE REPAY, AS WE PROMISED.

THE MAGICIAN PUTS HIS HAND ON THE STEEL ...

SSSSSSSSS

AND VANISHES INTO THE RISING SMOKE.

'LYRA, ARE YOU ALL RIGHT?

I HEARD YOU SPEAKING...

HERE'S THE ANVIL THEY PROMISED.

I DON'T WANT IT.

WE'VE PAID TOO MUCH TO REFUSE IT!

I CAN'T FORGET THE FACES ON... THAT THING.

HERE, THERE'S A MARK ON IT.

LIKE YOUR CARDS.

IS IT GOOD FORTUNE OR BAD?

IT IS A FINE PLACE FOR A DISCREET EXCHANGE, AND TO IT, THROUGH NO COINCIDENCE AT ALL, COMES LIRAIN'S LOVER, THE HELL-HOUND, BOURNE.

HE FOLLOWS HIS INSTRUCTIONS CAREFULLY.

STOWING HIS SWORD...

SHOWING THE SILVER...

STANDING CLEAR OF THE HORSE.

VERY GOOD. NOW GET ON YOUR HORSE AND GO HOME.

I WILL NOT. YOU HAVE SOMETHING FOR ME.

WALK OVER TO THE WALL AND LOOK TOWARD SANCTUARY.

I WILL WALK TO THE WALL AND WATCH THE SADDLEBAGS, INSTEAD.

GOOD, YOU DIDN'T FORGET TO BRING IT.

GET BACK TO YOUR HORSE, THEN. I'LL PUT THE ROD DOWN WHEN I PICK UP THE MONEYBAGS.

THE HELL-HOUND SHRUGS AND DOES AS HE IS TOLD.

HANSE, THINKING HE'S VERY CLEVER INDEED, LOSES NO TIME IN MAKING THE EXCHANGE.

EVERYTHING GOES ACCORDING TO PLAN...

BUT NOT, UNFORTUNATELY, ACCORDING TO *HIS* PLAN.

WHILE HANSE STRUGGLES WITH THE DEAD WEIGHT OF THE SILVER, BOURNE PRODUCES AN ARM'S LENGTH OF STEEL FROM THE DEPTHS OF HIS MAILCOAT.

48

IT ISN'T EASY, BUT HANSE KEEPS HIS BALANCE AND HEADS FOR THE HORSE.

HE LEAPS ONTO A BOULDER AND FROM THERE TO THE HORSE'S BACK— JUST LIKE HE'S SEEN OTHERS DO.

BUT SHADOWSPAWN HAS NEVER MOUNTED A HORSE BEFORE...

...AND INEXPERIENCE AND THE WEIGHT OF HIS RANSOM CARRIES HIM RIGHT OFF THE OTHER SIDE.

HANSE TRIES A THROW THAT WORKED FINE WHEN HE WAS POORER.

BOURNE MANAGES TO DODGE THE KNIFE, BUT NOT HIS OWN HORSE.

SEIZING THE OPPORTUNITY AND THE MONEYBAGS, HANSE MAKES HIS ESCAPE.

PERHAPS HE SHOULD HAVE DONE SOMETHING ABOUT BUYING OFF A GOD OR TWO.

PERHAPS HE SHOULD HAVE VISITED THE RUINS WHILE THE SUN STILL SHONE.

HE CERTAINLY SHOULD HAVE TAKEN NOTE OF THAT DARK, ROUND SHADOW—

AND NOT RUN HEADLONG INTO THE WELL.

CRASH
BAM
SPLOOSH!

THE THIEF IS ALIVE... AND WET AND POOR AGAIN.

51

AWPGH-H-H

SO MUCH FOR *THAT* HOPE.

LINGFF!

HANSE HEARS THE FADING SOUNDS OF SOMEONE RUNNING AWAY.

HELLO DOWN THERE!

I AM PRINCE KADAKITHIS. I HAVE THE SAVANKH.

PERHAPS I SPEAK USELESSLY TO ONE DEAD OR DYING.

PERHAPS NOT, IN WHICH CASE YOU MAY REMAIN THERE AND DIE SLOWLY... OR BE DRAWN UP TO DIE UNDER TORTURE...

...OR YOU CAN AGREE TO HELP ME IN A LITTLE PLAN I'VE JUST DEVISED.

WELL— SPEAK UP!

I'M YOUR TOOL... ER, *MAN.*

HANSE AGREES TO THE PRINCE'S PLAN... AND FINDS HIMSELF AT THE MERCY OF HIS ENEMY!

NO SENSE LEAVIN' HIM A *WHOLE* MAN...

NO NEED TO TORTURE HIM THERE... YET.

SURELY HE'S NOT *TALL* ENOUGH...?

WELL, DO *SOMETHING* TO HIM.

WHIFF— SNAP!

OH!

WHIPPIN' A MAN'S NOT TO MY STYLE.

I'D RATHER REARRANGE HIS ARMS A BIT.

STAY THERE— I'LL TURN THE CRANK FOR YOU.

WAIT...

I'LL TALK—

AND TALK HE DOES. HE TELLS THEM ABOUT HIMSELF AND ABOUT BOURNE AND LIRAIN—EXACTLY AS THE PRINCE HAD TOLD HIM.

REMEMBER—THE PRINCE-GOVERNOR IS MERCIFUL.

...AND NOT QUITE AS DUMB AS HE SEEMS.

O-O-O-H.

DAMN!

CAN I GO HOME NOW?

SOON THE PRINCE AND THE HELL-HOUNDS ZALBAR AND ARMAN ARE STANDING OUTSIDE THE DOOR TO LIRAIN'S CHAMBER.

DO WAIT HERE. I'M HANDLING THIS ALONE.

BUT—

THAT'S AN ORDER, CAPTAIN.

IF THAT IDIOT GETS HIMSELF KILLED...

YOU CAN COME IN NOW.

CLEAN IT UP.

YESSIR.

YESSIR.

NOT BAD AT ALL...

I DON'T BELIEVE IT.

54

ONE-THUMB LIKES THE DAWNLIGHT.

IT IS HARD, *REVEALING* RATHER THAN CLEANSING. DECADENT, STALE, WORN, MORTAL. HE TAKES DARK PLEASURE IN IT...

DOUBLE PLEASURE, THIS MORNING, A SLIGHT *KRRF* OVERDOSE SINGING DEATHSONG IN HIS BRAIN.

ANY TROUBLE, ONE-THUMB?

NO TROUBLE. NO *KRRF*, EITHER.

IT MUST STILL BE GOING ON. IF MIZRAITH HAD LOST, I'D KNOW, I THINK.

OR IF HE'D WON?

HE THINKS ABOUT MIZRAITH. THINKS ABOUT VISITING THE MAGE. HE'S BEEN CAUTIOUS FOR OVER A DAY.

POSSIBLY. I'LL BE IN TOUCH WITH YOUR MISTRESS ONCE I HAVE SOMETHING FOR HER.

BEFORE HE REACHES THE BOTTOM OF THE STAIRS, HE KNOWS SOMETHING IS WRONG. VERY WRONG.

55

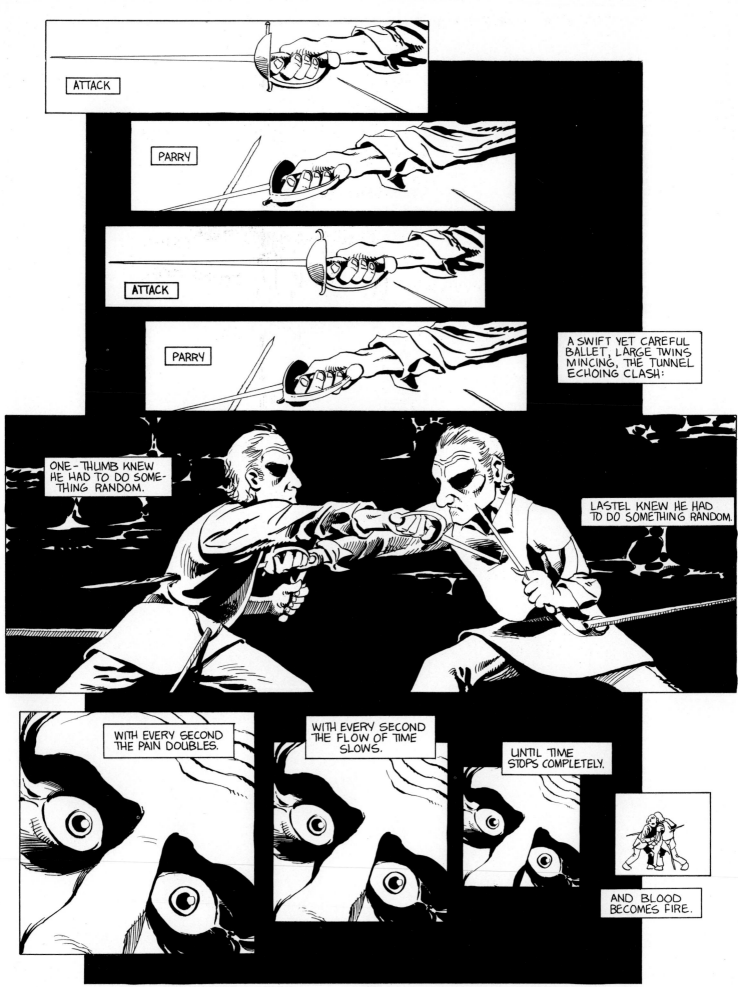

59

60

62

63

Afterword

BEHIND THE SCENES IN THIEVES' WORLD...

It has been pointed out to me that while the readers of the regular **Thieves' World** anthologies are familiar with how the series started, our newer readers of the graphic form remain blissfully in the dark.

Like so many ideas, **Thieves' World** was born at a science fiction convention, specifically Boskone in 1978. For the unaware, these conventions (approximately 300 a year in the continental U.S. alone) are gatherings of authors, artists, editors, and fans, highlighted by a few panel discussions and *lots* of informal conversations. One of the major reasons for attending is a chance for the various professionals to meet, greet, and compare notes with their colleagues from around the country. Thus it was that Thursday night found Gordie (Gordon R.) Dickson, Lynn Abbey, and me enjoying a quiet dinner at the hotel restaurant prior to the madness of the convention proper. The conversation ranged from the current market to projects in progress, and finally settled on pet peeves in writing. Fortified by the dinner wine, I waded into the fray with two of my favorite gripes.

First, it annoys me that there is very little suspense in a heroic fantasy series. I mean, however desperate a scrape Conan has gotten himself into this time, you know before reaching the end of the episode that he's going to emerge intact, if for no other reason than that there are five more volumes to go. It's a rough problem to beat, because the favored format for heroic fantasy *is* a series, which got me into my second complaint.

To enter the heroic fantasy field invariably means the author is doomed to reinvent the wheel. That is, even though Howard detailed the Hyborian Age and Leiber set up the marvelous town of Lankhmar, any new writer has to scratch-build a universe before he or she can start writing in the field. Now if you think this is an easy task, that "in fantasy, anything goes," you haven't ever tried it. Everything from geology to ecology has to be considered, along with anthropology and political science, with little things like magic systems and weapons technology thrown in for laughs. I mean, we're trying to create a whole world here, folks, and that means monetary systems and fashion design if the image is going to be complete and consistent. The job is so monumental that, once constructed, it is easier to continue writing stories in one's established universe than it is to junk it and start from scratch with another...hence the tendency toward series.

Along with the exclusive universes, it occurred to me that there were marvelous characters living in the pages of works sharing the same bookshelf that would never meet. What if....

What if Fafhrd and the Mouser pulled one of their famous heists? Doubling back on their trail, they send the pursuing mob off in the wrong direction. Well and good, end story...

unless....

Unless coming down the street into the teeth of the mob is Conan with his saddlebags full of loot from another unrelated caper!

What if Kane and Elric took jobs marshalling armies on *opposite sides of the same war?*

The possibilities become endless.

This idea was batted around the table, until I finally admitted that I had a plan in the back of my mind to write a multi-character series. My thought was to write a series of short pieces, each centering around one of several characters living on the same street in a less-than-reputable town. Probably, they would not know each other but would occasionally note the existence of antics of the others in their own stories. The advantage of this system would be that the main focus would be the setting, the street, and I could abruptly kill off any given character if the spirit moved me. Of course, my time was already committed to other projects, so this one would have to wait until I had a clear block of time to do the idea justice.

Then Gordie came up with the fateful suggestion: Why not franchise the idea? I wanted different characters; what could be more varied than having different authors handle the various viewpoints? As long as I maintained control for continuity, we could all play in the same sandbox. Thus **Thieves' World** came into existence.

I think it is tribute to the amount of wine we had been drinking that, at the time, it sounded like a good idea. Looking back after eight years, I could throttle Gordie over the "all I have to do is control it" toss-off. Even after recruiting Lynn to share the editorial duties, **Thieves' World** has grown to a point where it takes a majority of our time to manage it. Instead of simply building our own world, we have to ride herd on a small army of creative minds, each set on adding his or her own particular flourish in universe building. You can see the characters fight...well, so do the authors, with Lynn and me caught in the crossfire as referees.

The final winner, however, is the reader. Regardless of how we got here, the combined talents of the authors have created a city and a cast of characters which simply could not spring from a single mind. While it's interesting to get occasional glimpses "behind the scenes," the important thing is the result. The entire **Thieves' World** team sincerely hopes that the readers derive a fraction of the enjoyment reading these works as we got from putting them together.

Robert Lynn Asprin
January 1986
Ann Arbor, Michigan